For Mat, and helpful cups of tea in the early hours
- O H

For Linda, my creative guardian angel. Her generosity has
helped me sleep a little better at night. Thank you
- C P

LITTLE TIGER PRESS LTD.
an imprint of the Little Tiger Group
1 The Coda Centre, 189 Munster Road, London SW6 6AW
www.littletiger.co.uk

First published in Great Britain 2017

Text by Owen Hart
Text copyright © Little Tiger Press 2017
Illustrations copyright © Caroline Pedler 2017
Caroline Pedler has asserted her right to be identified as the illustrator
of this work under the Copyright, Designs and Patents Act, 1988
A CIP catalogue record for this book is available from the British Library

Printed in China • LTP/1400/1809/0217

2 4 6 8 10 9 7 5 3 1

I Can't Sleep!

Owen Hart • Caroline Pedler

LITTLE TIGER

LONDON

It was the middle of the night.
All was quiet on board the *Leaping Salmon*.
But Mole couldn't sleep.

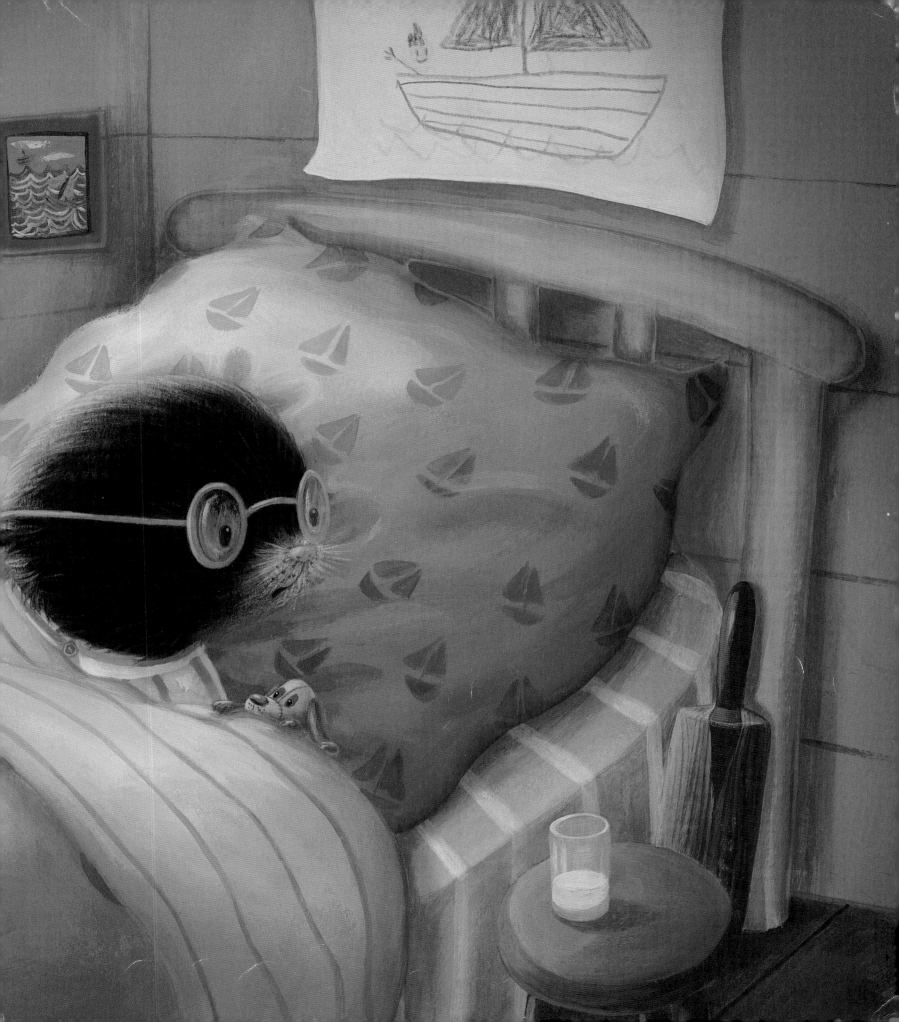

"Fiddlesticks!" he sighed.
And he pattered across the
deck and creaked open
Mouse's door.

"Mouse! Mouse!" he called. "I can't sleep.
Can I come in here with you?"
    Mouse yawned and peered at Mole in the moonlight.
"Come on, then," he said. "Don't forget your bedding."

While Mole plumped
up the pillows,
Mouse had an idea.
"Let's try a bedtime story,"
he said happily.
"Yippee!" cheered Mole.

Mouse turned the pages and
Mole began to feel sleepy.
But all too soon they reached
the Happy Ever After.
"It's too short!" said Mole.
"Please can we have another?"

Mole picked a second book, and Mouse began to read.
But then Mole gave a sudden squeak.
"Too scary!" he cried.
"This won't help me sleep!"

So Mouse read a third story,
about a boat just like theirs.
"Ahhh," sighed Mole. "It's just right."
And he settled down to sleep.

But Mole wasn't
quiet for long.
"Mouse! Mouse!"
he called.
"I still can't sleep!"

"Why not?" asked Mouse.
"It's too dark!" said Mole.
"And I can't stop thinking about the scary story."

Mouse turned on the
bedside lamp. A soft
glow filled the room
and soon Mole was
silent again.

But only for a while.
"Mouse!" he cried. "Now it's too bright!"

Luckily, Mouse had a better idea.
He opened the cupboard above his bed
and brought down a large piece of paper.
"That won't help me sleep!" said Mole.
"Watch . . ." said Mouse.

Mouse began to
snip the paper.
Mole looked on
in wonder.

With a tuck
and a fold,
Mouse had
made the
perfect
night light.

"Wow – look at that!" said Mole as stars
and moons danced on the walls. "It's just right."
And he rolled over with a happy sigh.

But Mole didn't settle for long.
"Mouse! Mouse!" he called.
"I STILL can't sleep. I'm too cold!"

Mouse looked in the
drawer beneath his bed
and brought out
a warm blanket.
"Have this," he said.
Mole pulled the blanket
right up to his chin and
closed his tired eyes.

"Mouse!"
he squeaked.
"Now I'm too hot!"
"Even without the
blanket?" asked Mouse.
"Yes!" fretted Mole.

So Mouse had his
best idea of all.
"But I'll need your
help," he told Mole.
Together, they shifted
the chair . . .

and dragged the
dresser . . .

and tugged at
the trunk.

With one last push, the bed was in
place next to the open window.
"That's just right," said Mole.
"Thank you, Mouse."
And he snuggled down once more.

At last all was peaceful.
The river lapped gently.
A frog croaked softly.
And everything was quiet
aboard the *Leaping Salmon*.

But not for long . . .

"Mole! Mole!"
called Mouse.
"I can't sleep!"

It wasn't too dark
or too light.

And it wasn't too
hot or too cold.

Whatever could be wrong?

"STOP THAT SNORING!"

"Mole!" cried Mouse.